April

t

tate publishing
CHILDREN'S DIVISION

The
Girlsprouts

Published by Tate Publishing & Enterprises, LLC
127 E. Trade Center Terrace | Mustang, Oklahoma 73064 USA
1.888.361.9473 | www.tatepublishing.com

Tate Publishing is committed to excellence in the publishing industry. The company reflects the philosophy established by the founders, based on Psalm 68:11,
"The Lord gave the word and great was the company of those who published it."

Book design copyright © 2012 by Tate Publishing, LLC. All rights reserved.
Cover and interior design by Errol Villamante
Illustrations by Noelle Barcelo

Published in the United States of America

ISBN: 978-1-62295-247-2
1. Juvenile Fiction / Social Issues / Self-Esteem & Self-Reliance
2. Juvenile Fiction / Animals / Butterflies, Moths & Caterpillars
12.11.15

"For I know the thoughts that I think toward you," says the Lord, "thoughts of peace and not of evil, to give you a future and a hope."

Jeremiah 29:11

dedication

This book is dedicated to Hannah. Without your imagination and participation, this book would not exist. I thank God for trusting me with such a precious opportunity...being your mom.

chapter 1

Springtime was in the air! The winter had been long and hard, but the new season always brought new life and hope. All the bugs were busy at their chores, and Miss Ladybug was preparing for the Girlsprout troop's seed drive.

As she scurried to the meeting place, the sandbox in the back yard, Miss Ladybug could feel the excitement of the community. All the flowers were blooming, and the air was fresh and crisp.

When she arrived, she saw her girls talking excitedly, telling of their adventures since they were last together. When they saw her, their excitement grew. Miss Ladybug was so kind and loving to them; they were anxious to hear what awaited this season.

chapter 2

"Happy springtime!" exclaimed Miss Ladybug. "I am overjoyed to see you in good health. Gather round now. I have a surprise for you."

Butterbean, a round, lumpy caterpillar, clumsily made her way into the corner. She was quickly followed by Flower, a spritely little bumblebee. They were best friends, despite their differences. "What could the surprise be?" whispered Flower excitedly.

"I cannot imagine," said Butterbean, "but I hope it tastes good! All my leaves are stale after such a long winter."

"I know," said Flower, "I cannot wait for fresh pollen!"

"Quiet, girls, quiet! Our troop has a new member. You can join us now, Sugar," Miss Ladybug said kindly.

From behind a pail came a shy, little ant. She was very beautiful and was a graceful bug. As she neared them, she became more timid.

"Don't worry, we don't sting," said Flower. "Come on over."

As Sugar joined the others with Miss Ladybug, she finally felt like she belonged.

chapter 3

At the meeting, they discussed the fundraisers. The girls were to sell as many Girlsprout seeds as they could to go to the harvest festival that year.

"We will sell sunflower seeds, mustard seeds, and cocoa beans," said Miss Ladybug. As you know, the harvest festival is a wonderful time of fun, food, and games, so do your best."

The girls got right to work. They worked very hard, selling the seeds to family and friends, asking everyone they knew. Flower had a lot of business at the hive. All the bees were very supportive. Sugar managed to sell twice as much as Flower. Butterbean's attempt, however, wasn't that productive. It was not because she didn't try. As a caterpillar, she was pretty much on her own. She ended the week very discouraged.

"I am such a failure," said Butterbean. "I can never do anything right!"

"Oh, Butter, that's not true! You are the best at being my friend, and I don't know anyone who can eat more leaves faster than you can!" said Flower.

"Well, look where that has gotten me! I am big, lumpy, and slow!" said Butterbean with tears in her eyes.

"I think you are great, Butter!" exclaimed Sugar.

"Look , Sugar! You are a beautiful, bright color. Flower, your wings make you fly, and so fast! Miss Ladybug, you're the best of all. I'll always be just a worm!"

With that, Butterbean sulked home, feeling sorrier and sorrier as she went.

chapter 4

The next meeting came, and everyone began gathering at the sandbox. Everyone except for Butterbean. The Girlsprouts were all very surprised. Butterbean never missed a meeting.

"This is not like Butter," said Flower. "Maybe something has happened."

"At our last meeting, she was very hard on herself. I am concerned," said Miss Ladybug. "We must look for her! Flower, you fly over the yard and tell everyone that Butter is missing. Sugar, you search the ground and spread the news that way. If anyone knows anything, tell them to report to me immediately. Girls, we cannot stop until we find her!"

chapter 5

Flower buzzed around the yard, alerting everyone about Butter. Sugar journeyed through the tall grass and shrubs, looking everywhere. Miss Ladybug also searched and searched.

This went on for two weeks with no word and no sign of Butterbean. The Girlsprouts began to think they would never find their friend.

"We might have to give up!" sobbed Sugar. "We've looked everywhere!"

"We will never give up!" said Miss Ladybug. "The Girlsprouts always stick together."

There was a rustling of wings as Mr. Robin landed in the sandbox. Mr. Robin was a nosey, old bird, and he knew everything about the yard.

"I hear you girls are missing someone. She's been gone for two weeks?" he asked.

"Yes," said Miss Ladybug. "It's Butterbean, a big green caterpillar that we love so much!"

"Green, ay? And a caterpillar, you say? I think I know what happened to your friend," said Mr. Robin. "But I'd rather show you than tell you. Climb on up. Flying is much faster."

Miss Ladybug and Sugar climbed on Mr. Robin's back, and they were off. Flower flew close behind.

chapter 6

Through the air they flew, to the tree beside the house. Sugar was quite rattled, for this was her first time in the air. She was glad to be off Mr. Robin's back.

"I think I'll stick to the ground from now on," said a shaking Sugar. "Is this where you saw Butter?"

"Wait a minute! I never said I saw her," replied Mr. Robin. "I said I think I know what happened to her. Look just over there, through those leaves."

Miss Ladybug, Sugar, and Flower peered through some leaves. Hanging from a branch was a lumpy little cocoon. The silk was wound thick, but Butterbean's green was shining through.

"I should have realized," said Miss Ladybug. "Butter has been undergoing a wonderful transformation."

"What kind of transformation?" asked Sugar.

Before anyone could answer, the cocoon began to twist and shake. Out popped Butterbean's chubby little head.

"What's all the noise about?" she asked groggily. "Can't you see I'm napping?"

As Butterbean wiggled to free herself from her cocoon, she did not notice everyone staring at her with amazement. She still felt like the same old worm. Were things ever going to look up for her?

chapter 7

"Oh, Butter! How wonderful!" said Flower, "Now we really can do everything together! We can gather pollen and flit across the yard!"

"I have never seen such beautiful colors ," said Sugar. "You're the loveliest insect in the whole yard!"

"What are you talking about? I must be dreaming," said Butterbean.

Miss Ladybug told Butterbean how they searched the last two weeks. She told her how Flower and Sugar had dedicated every day to finding her. Nothing was more important to the Girlsprouts than sticking together.

Next, she told Butter to turn and look in the window. Butter was delighted to see that while she was in her cocoon, beautiful wings had grown from her back. She began to cry tears of joy, for she had never known the beauty she possessed.

She sighed. "Oh my!" "I'm not sure I can use these things. They feel quite strange."

"Just concentrate," said Flower. "You can do anything you set your mind to."

"You can do it, Butter," encouraged Miss Ladybug. "I believe in you!"

Butterbean began to focus. The more she thought about flying through the air, the more her wings fluttered. Soon she had taken off and was laughing and flying around the tree. She had never felt more beautiful in her life.

e|LIVE

listen|imagine|view|experience

AUDIO BOOK DOWNLOAD INCLUDED WITH THIS BOOK!

In your hands you hold a complete digital entertainment package. In addition to the paper version, you receive a free download of the audio version of this book. Simply use the code listed below when visiting our website. Once downloaded to your computer, you can listen to the book through your computer's speakers, burn it to an audio CD or save the file to your portable music device (such as Apple's popular iPod) and listen on the go!

How to get your free audio book digital download:

1. Visit www.tatepublishing.com and click on the elLIVE logo on the home page.
2. Enter the following coupon code:
   84d5-31ab-b180-9453-5468-73b8-669f-ca1d
3. Download the audio book from your elLIVE digital locker and begin enjoying your new digital entertainment package today!